Here's how to make first-time reading easy and fun:

▶ Read the introduction at the beginning of each story aloud. Look through the pictures together so that your child can see what happens in the story before reading the words.

▶ Read one or two pages to your child, placing your finger under each word.

▶ Let your child touch the words and read the rest of the story. Give him or her time to figure out each new word.

▶ If your child gets stuck on a word, you might say, *"Try something. Look at the picture. What would make sense?"*

▶ If your child is still stuck, supply the right word. This will allow him or her to continue to read and enjoy the story. You might say, *"Could this word be 'ball'?"*

▶ Always praise your child. Praise what he or she reads correctly, and praise good tries too.

▶ Give your child lots of chances to read the story again and again. The more your child reads, the more confident he or she will become.

▶ Have fun!

Copyright © 2009 by Kathy Caple

First edition 2009

Library of Congress Cataloging-in-Publication Data is available.

Library of Congress Catalog Card Number 2009923262

ISBN 978-0-7636-3896-2

2 4 6 8 10 9 7 5 3 1

Printed in China

This book was typeset in Letraset Arta.
The illustrations were done in
watercolor and gouache.

Candlewick Press
99 Dover Street
Somerville, Massachusetts 02144

visit us at www.candlewick.com

TERMITE TALES

CANDLEWICK PRESS

Kathy Caple

Contents

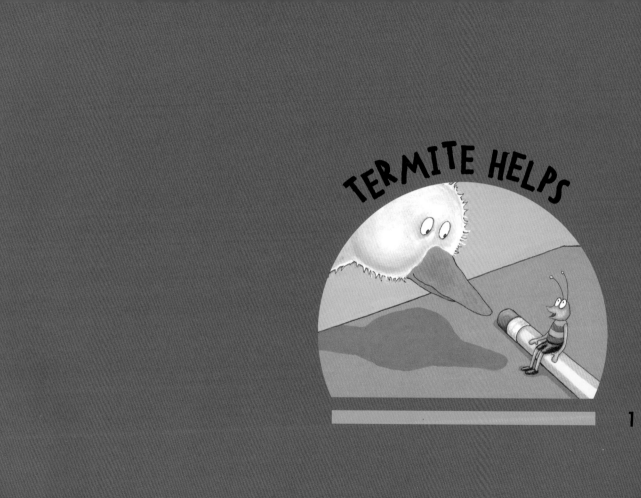

TERMITE HELPS

1

Introduction

This story is called *Termite Helps*.
It's about how Ostrich writes with a pencil,
and Termite sharpens it by eating the tip.
Soon it gets too small.

3

Ostrich writes with a pencil.

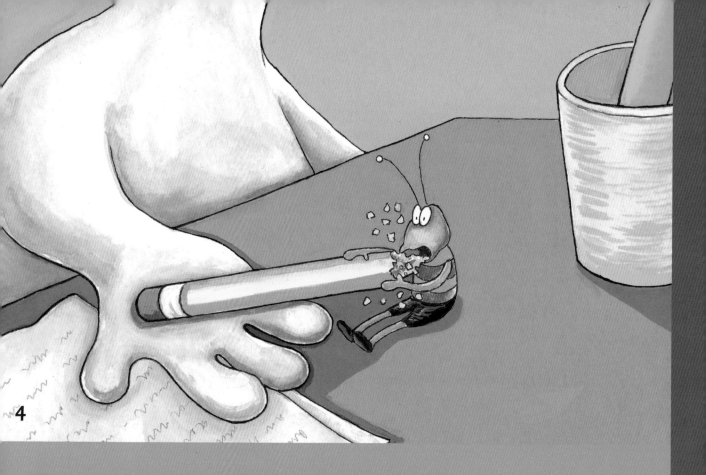

4

Termite sharpens the pencil.

5

Ostrich writes with a pencil.

6

Termite sharpens the pencil.

Ostrich writes and writes.

8

Termite sharpens and sharpens.

The pencil is all gone!

Ostrich writes with a pen.

TERMITE TAPS

Introduction

This story is called *Termite Taps*.
It's about how Termite tap-dances.
When he does a split, he rips his pants!

13

Termite tap-dances up the stairs.

14

Termite tap-dances down the stairs.

Termite tap-dances on a chair.

Termite tap-dances on a table.

Termite leaps to the floor.

click.

18

Termite clicks his heels.

Termite does a split. *RIP!*

20

Termite tap-dances backward!

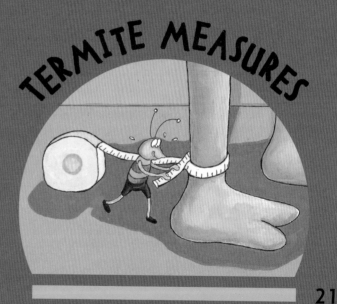

TERMITE MEASURES

21

Introduction

This story is called *Termite Measures*.
It's about how Termite measures Ostrich's
head, neck, wing, middle, leg, and ankle.
When he tries to measure Ostrich's foot,
he almost gets stepped on!

Termite measures Ostrich's head.

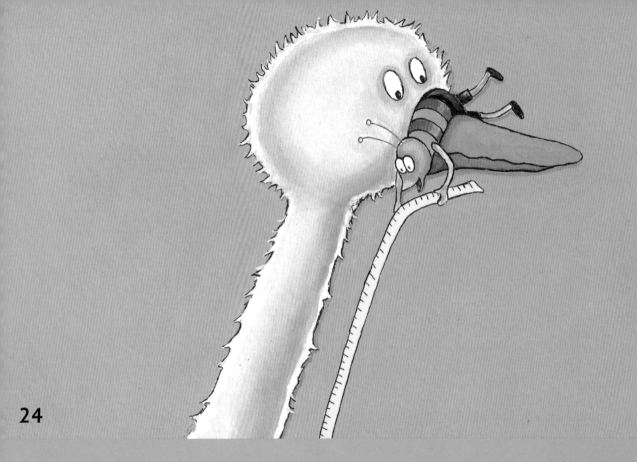

24

Termite measures Ostrich's neck.

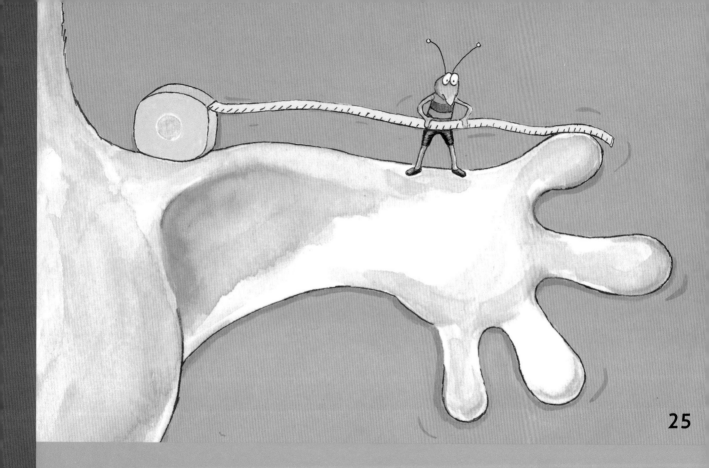

25

Termite measures Ostrich's wing.

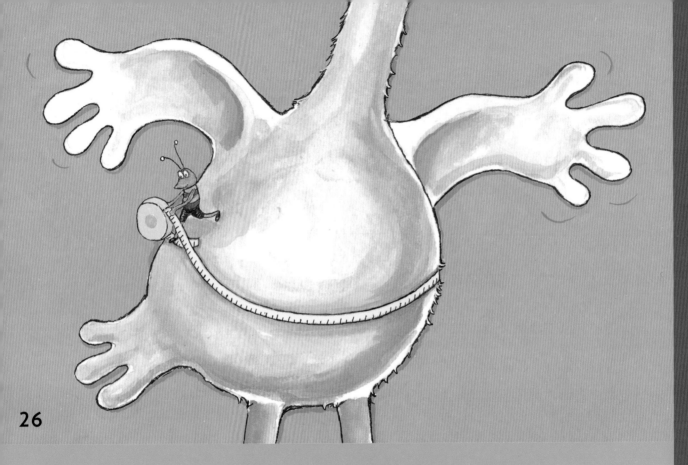

Termite measures Ostrich's middle.

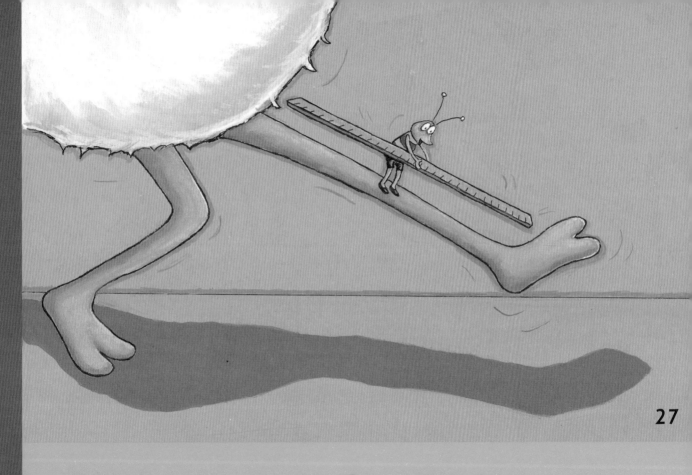

Termite measures Ostrich's leg.

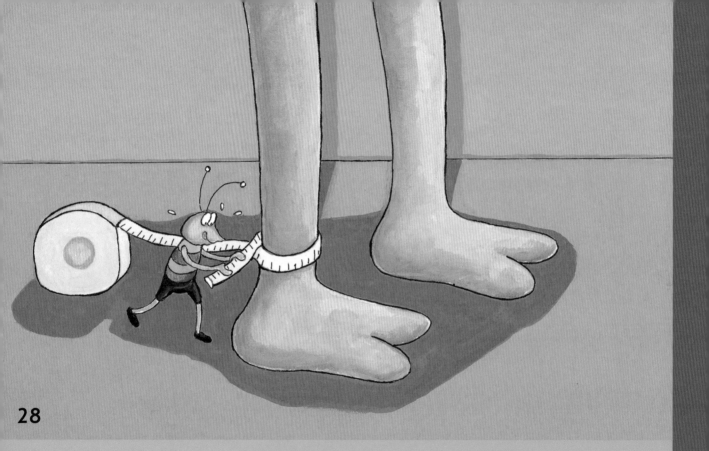

Termite measures Ostrich's ankle.

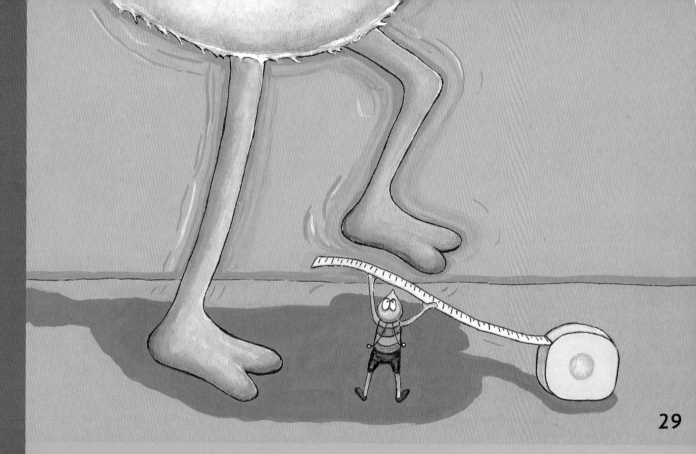

Termite tries to measure Ostrich's foot.

Termite gets out of Ostrich's way!

TERMITE IN THE CANOE

Introduction

This story is called *Termite in the Canoe*. It's about how Ostrich paddles the canoe while Termite eats a hole in it. When the canoe springs a leak, Ostrich and Termite have to swim.

Ostrich paddles the canoe.

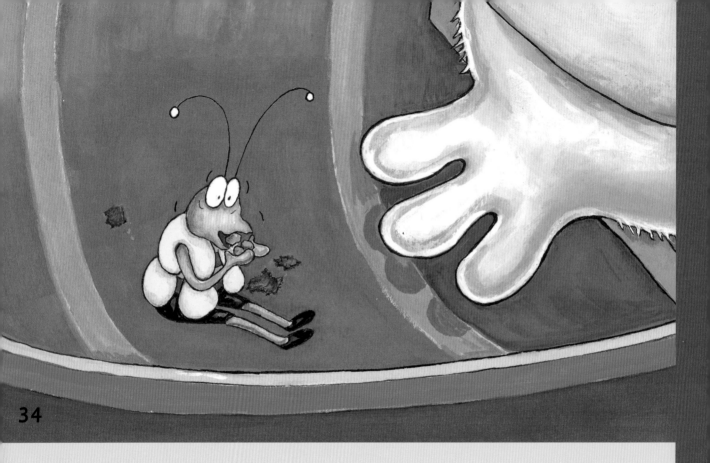

Termite nibbles the canoe.

Ostrich paddles the canoe.

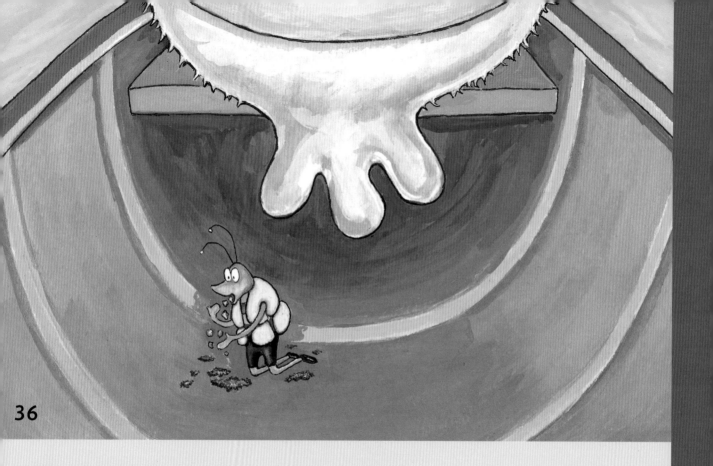

36

Termite nibbles the canoe.

Ostrich paddles and paddles.

Termite nibbles and nibbles.

39

The canoe springs a leak.

Ostrich and Termite swim.